Dealing with Bullies

Om KIDZ
An imprint of Om Books International

It was Monday morning and Anna's family was in time for breakfast.

'What are you going to do today in school, Annie?' Anna's father asked.

Anna remained silent, playing around with the food on her plate.

Seeing her disinterest, he coaxed her gently.

'It's Sally, Daddy,' said Anna.

'Don't let her get to you, Annie,' he said, thoughtfully. 'Play with the friends who like you. You don't need to let her bother you.'

'Hey bug-eyes! What do you have in your lunchbox today? Worms?' Jeered Sally.

Sally's friends, who surrounded her, giggled.

'Leave me alone!' Anna exclaimed.

But Sally pushed her over and walked away laughing.

Anna's glasses flew off, and she bruised her knee. Max and Lia rushed to help her up, while Ben dusted off her glasses and handed them to her.

Ben wished Anna could push Sally back. He loved his friend and was angry with Sally.

They had art class with Mrs. Brown and music class with Mr. Ross. Anna and her friends had a wonderful time and soon forgot all about Sally.

At lunch, Anna and Max opened their lunch boxes together. Both had cheese sandwiches that they loved. But before Anna could bite into her sandwich, Sally and her friends walked by and knocked it off the table.

`Oops!´ She said with a wicked smile.

Max jumped up to shove her, but Anna stopped him.

She did not want to be like Sally. Max was angry with her for stopping him.

They walked back to class gloomily.

Mrs. Brown had an exciting announcement that afternoon that cheered them up. `Children, for tomorrow's show and tell, I want you to bring your favourite soft toys. You could bring your plants to class too, so that we can all learn a bit more about each other.'

`Yay!' The class broke into a cheer!

At bath time that night, Daddy noticed the scrape on Anna's knee. 'Hey Anna-Banana, how did you hurt your knee?' He asked.

'Daddy, please don't tell Mommy, or she will worry. Sally pushed me at school today. I ignored her, just like you told me to. Max says I should have pushed her back,' she said.

`Well, I think you did the right thing. I'm very proud of you. But you know what, Annie,' Daddy said as he towelled her dry. `You don't like Sally because she hits and is mean to people. You hitting her back will not solve this problem. Because you are not her. You are lucky you are loved by friends and family genuinely. Maybe she is not getting the same attention. Be kind.'

Daddy thought he would have a word with Mommy and Mrs. Brown later.

The next day, Anna walked into class with her well-loved twin toy hippos, Tweedledum and Tweedledee. The classroom looked like a little zoo! Except for one naughty girl, everyone had brought their soft toys or potted plants.

Sally came with her fluffy white cat. Walking over to Anna, she said, 'My Cleo would like to meet your hippos. They'd make such a tasty bite!'

Just then, Ben shrieked loudly behind them on seeing the cat. Cleo yowled in terror and leapt out of Sally's arms. Out of the classroom window she shot, fast as an arrow!

Cleo had scooted up the tallest tree in the playground. There she was on the highest branch!

Sally threw a tantrum when she could not reach Cleo. Then she stood there, crying helplessly. `Come down, please, Cleo. Will somebody help, please?' The class stood around watching–no one was brave enough to climb that high.

`Cleo's just frightened, Sally,' said Anna. `I have an idea.'

Anna ran to Mrs. Brown and asked for some milk in a dish, so she could tempt Cleo to come down from the tree. Sally needed help!

Anna ran back to the field with the milk. The trick worked. Cleo came down to the relief of the crowd and slurped the milk happily.

Sally threw her arms around Anna and hugged her. `Thank you, Anna. I'm sorry I was so mean to you,' she said, sheepishly. `Can we be friends?'

`Gladly!' Said Anna, smiling. Happy to be friends, they walked back to class.

Sally, Anna and all their friends are now known for being the most cheerful and helpful group in school. Daddy was right. You can be strong by being kind and standing up for yourself and others.